Family Storybook Library

The Heart Is the Strongest Muscle

Stories About Courage and Responsibility

BOOK EIGHT

First Edition
1 3 5 7 9 10 8 6 4 2

ISBN: 0-7868-5873-7

The Heart Is the Strongest Muscle

Stories About Courage and Responsibility

Introduction

Courage and quick thinking are required on the battlefield, but everyday living also often calls for inner strength. Courage can be found in both grand gestures and in quiet moments. Everyone lauds a returning hero, but we must also remember and honor the anonymous sacrifices of many. Standing up for what is right, not just going along with the crowd, staying true to important values; these acts require tremendous strength of character.

Mulan demonstrates courage and cunning when she outwits the enemy in "Mulan Saves the Day." Although her act is much quieter, the church mouse's wife provides hope for many in "A Gift Greater Than Gold."

Mulan Saves the Day

from *Mulan*

⎯⎯⎯∞⎯⎯⎯

There are many ways to fight,
but the best is with your brain.

t the Tung-Shao Pass, high in the snow-covered peaks of China, the Huns attacked Captain Shang and his troops without warning. Hundreds of flaming arrows descended on Shang's men from somewhere up the mountain.

"Get out of range!" Shang cried. "Save the cannons!"

The soldiers carried the cannons back behind some rocks and aimed them at the enemy.

"Fire!" Shang shouted.

Mulan, disguised as a man, fired a cannon at the snipers above her.

The rockets exploded, and the Huns fired back with more arrows. Mulan and the other soldiers ducked.

"Hold the last cannon!" Shang commanded. His troops waited, peering through the haze. The mountains were silent.

As the smoke cleared, Mulan and the

others gasped. On top of the ridge, along the entire horizon, stretched a massive line of Huns. In front rode Shan-Yu, the Hun leader.

In a firm, solemn voice, Shang ordered, "Prepare to fight. If we die, we die with honor."

"Hee-yah!" cried Shan-Yu, charging down the mountain with his troops.

"Yao!" Shang shouted to one of his men.

"Aim the last cannon at Shan-Yu!"

Mulan stood beside Yao, her sword drawn. She looked down at her blade and saw the mountain reflected in its shiny surface. She gazed up at the mountain, then at the charging Huns.

Quickly Mulan sheathed her sword and grabbed the cannon away from Yao.

"Ping!" called Shang, using the man's name Mulan had invented to disguise herself. "Come back! Ping!"

As Shan-Yu galloped toward her, Mulan carried the cannon up the mountain. Suddenly she stopped. She placed the cannon in front of Shan-Yu, then tilted the barrel toward the top of the mountain.

Mulan fired, and the rocket sailed over Shan-Yu's head. It lodged in the overhanging

mountaintop, then
exploded with a
thunderous roar,
causing a massive
avalanche.

As the wall of
snow spilled toward
Shan-Yu, the Hun
leader glared at
Mulan. He had been
outwitted! And by
an ordinary soldier,
no less. Shan-Yu
slashed at Mulan,
but she hurried away,
eager to escape the
monstrous force
rumbling down the

mountain. The avalanche overtook Shan-Yu and his men, and the Huns were defeated.

A Gift Greater Than Gold

from *Robin Hood*

─────◦◦◦◦─────

The greatest gift you can give is hope.

Long ago in a town called Nottingham, England, the people found themselves struggling to survive. Good King Richard was away fighting in the Holy Land, and his brother, Prince John, ruled in his place.

Prince John was wicked. Fortunately, he was none too bright. But his first officer, the Sheriff of Nottingham, was even more wicked than Prince John—and he was sly as a fox.

Prince John wanted to raise the taxes—so he'd have more money to spend. He sent his

henchman, the
Sheriff, around
to the people
of Nottingham
to collect their
coins. The
Sheriff took
money even
from the poorest
people of the
village.

An outlaw
named Robin
Hood, along
with his band
of Merry Men,
tried their best
to make things

better for the poor of Nottingham. They spent their time stealing from the rich and spreading the wealth among the needy. But even they couldn't stop the cruel Sheriff from collecting taxes. His nose was so long, he could sniff out gold coins no matter

how well they were hidden. A more ruthless
tax collector there never was.

As the Sheriff carried out his tax campaign,
the poor of Nottingham became even poorer.

Hard times had come to Friar Tuck's
church, as well. The good priest was devoted
to giving money to the needy, but now his

collection box was empty. No one in the
village could spare so much as a penny.

One day Friar Tuck was thinking about
his next sermon—and trying to think of
something to say that would lift his

congregation's spirits—when he had two small visitors. He was happy to see that it was the church mouse and his wife. And what a pleasant shock they gave him.

"We were saving this coin for a rainy day," the church mouse's wife said, offering Friar Tuck a gold coin, "but the

sun no longer shines in Nottingham, so we want you to have it."

The kindness and generosity of these good creatures—who were poorer than anyone—brought tears to Friar Tuck's eyes.

He lovingly placed the coin in the collection box.

Now he knew

there was hope for Nottingham. For as long as such kind and loving people lived there, they would always find room in their hearts to help one another.

All will be well, Friar Tuck thought. Good King Richard would soon return. He could feel it in his bones.